# *CommuterLit*
# *SELECTIONS*
## *Fall 2013*
### A Month of Reading
### for Your Transit Commute

Published by CommuterLit via Lulu.com
Toronto, Ontario, Canada
commuterlit.com

Editing: Nancy Kay Clark
Design & Layout: Doug Bennet
Typeset in Baskerville & Gill Sans

Cover image: iStock


CommuterLit Selections Fall 2013:
A Month of Reading for Your Transit Commute


ISBN   978-0-9921070-0-0

# *Preface*

Welcome to this issue of *CommuterLit Selections Fall 2013*, the first of what will be periodic anthologies of poems and short stories culled from the best of *CommuterLit.com*.

*CommuterLit.com* is an ezine for readers like you — smart, interested in the world and on the go. *CommuterLit.com* posts a new short story, novel excerpt or poem each day from Monday to Friday, specially formatted to read on mobile devices of all screen sizes. Of course, you can also access the stories and poems from the *CommuterLit.com* website at any time. Or, if you prefer print, you can now purchase one of our anthologies. (Future anthologies will also be available as ebooks.)

Our focus is works of fiction, memoir or poetry that can be enjoyed during a 20- to 30-minute public-transit commute to work. And because we know your taste in reading material is varied and sophisticated, we surprise you by selecting samples of not only literary fiction, but sci fi, fantasy, horror, mystery, crime, romance and experimental combinations thereof.

**Want to spice up your daily reading?** Log on to *CommuterLit.com* every weekday morning for a new story or poem. Sign up to our Twitter feed @commuterlit for daily notices or our weekly email newsletter (sent every Monday) highlighting the upcoming week's posts and authors. Visit *CommuterLit.com* to sign up.

**Are you a writer or a poet?** We're always looking for compelling poems and stories to post. Visit *CommuterLit.com* for our Submission Guidelines.

Here's to a good read and a happy commute.

Nancy Kay Clark
*CommuterLit* publisher & editor

# TABLE *of* CONTENTS

**Week One**
*Week One Authors* 8

*Monday:* Commuter Train 9

*Tuesday:* Starlight 10

*Wednesday:* The Mystery of the Garbanzo Bean Morrocan 12

*Thursday:* Tyrant's Justice 14

*Friday:* Planting Flowers 17


**Week Two**
*Week Two Authors* 24

*Monday:* Stadium 25

*Tuesday:* Soldier's Last Wish 27

*Wednesday:* Consider the Suburbs II 30

*Thursday:* Time's a Wasting 32

*Friday:* Missile 34

## Week Three

*Week Three Authors*  42

*Monday:* Teaching  43

*Tuesday:* The Hall  44

*Wednesday:* Worm's eye View  48

*Thursday:* Crow Visits  51

*Friday:* Planned Obsolescence  52

## Week Four

*Week Four Authors*  56

*Monday:* Honour Thy Roots  57

*Tuesday:* Free at Last  61

*Wednesday:* Speak Softly  63

*Thursday:* Lotus  69

*Friday:* Hey Miles, What's the Plan?  70

# Week One

"Hiho! Hiho! It's off to work we go!"
— *The Seven Dwarves*

# Week One Authors

### Monday: Commuter Train

**Elizabeth Barnes** has been writing prose and poetry for over 20 years and is a member of the High Park Writers' Group in Toronto. In 2002 she was short-listed for the Writers' Union of Canada short story contest for "The Yellow Dahlia." She was published in *Canadian Voices, An Anthology of Prose and Poetry by Emerging Canadian Writers, Vols. One and Two* (Bookland Press) and in 2010 published *Giving into Gravity (*In Our Words), a poetry collection.

### Tuesday: Starlight

**Eirik Gumeny** is the author of two flash fiction chapbooks, *Boy Meets Girl* (Kattywompus Press, 2013) and *Storybook Romance* (Red Bird Chapbooks, 2013). He currently resides in New Mexico with his wife and a backyard full of plants he can't identify. **egumeny.com**

### Wednesday: The Mystery of the Garbanzo Bean Moroccan

Born and raised in Windsor, Ontario, **Dave Medd** has slowly crept in a general northeasterly direction since departing: Waterloo, Ontario (school), London, Ontario (more school) and Toronto (work and different work). He considers writing a hobby in the same sense that many consider gardening or golfing one: something to devote enjoyed time, hopefully get better at, but done predominantly for its own sake. Should a screenplay ever sell, however, then that was the plan all along.

### Thursday: Tyrant's Justice

**Brandon Crilly** is a high school history teacher and freelance editor from Ontario. His speculative fiction has been previously published in *That Not Forgotten* (Hidden Brook Press) and is forthcoming in *On Spec* and *The End* (Static Movement). **brandoncrilly.wordpress.com**

### Friday: Planting Flowers

**Celynne Grewe-Hinzmann** writes literary fiction, short stories, novellas and personal essays. She lives with her family in southern Ontario and is currently working on a novel.

# *Monday*
# COMMUTER TRAIN

## By Elizabeth Barnes

The commuter train dawdles
held back by a signal to go slow
where it usually hurtles through
with no time to waste

I am for once not buried and busy in a book
and observe a laneway to the right
— too quickly the train passes —
a flash of green with
a line of water and
on this overcast morning
the marshy waters fingering the feet of the
white birches
waiting to inhale

and I am gone into that line of water
bound hand and foot
attached root and stem          leaf and blossom
to mounds of marsh marigolds
the train abandoned      left to tear
its busy business way
into the downtown core

# *Tuesday*
# STARLIGHT

## By Eirik Gumeny

THERE SHOULDN'T be stars in Bushwick, but there they are. Dim and weak and falling, but there they are.

Maria looks down the avenue, at a dozen neighbours on a dozen tar-paper rooftops; a dozen sisters and brothers, broken down and staring straight up.

Maria breathes deep and pulls her sweater tighter, returns her gaze to the sky falling down around her. She tries to count the streaking starlight, to lose herself in the night and retreat from the world, from the voices and the footsteps, the rattling windows and the rumbling street, from the slamming doors and the thudding beds, the cigarettes and the shouting, from the dull heartbeat of the apartment.

"Star light, star bright... First star I see tonight..."

Maria wants to remember what it's like to sleep at night without the sound of sirens. To see a clear sky and not be astounded, to walk through grass without taking two trains. She wants carpets again, counters again, closets and cable television. She wants to remember when a studio only had to fit a drafting table, not a mattress and a microwave. She wants to draw for herself again, without client demands and agency deadlines.

"Wish I may, wish I might... Have this wish..."

Maria doesn't recognize her own dreams anymore. Doesn't believe in a future that she doesn't fear. She doesn't know how much longer she'll be able to stand beneath the weight of this city, beneath the concrete and the shadows, the crowds, the clamour, the fear, the fury, beneath the very weight of the air itself, without her knees being driven into the pavement.

She wants to remember why she came here, to New York, this city among all the others.

She wants to remember why she stays.

"I wish tonight…"

Maria's heart races and the city laughs.

She is no longer alone. Shoes crunch, voices murmur and cough. The rooftop trembles under the weight of the building's inhabitants. Her neighbours swarm around her — the girl from down the hall, the landlord, the dealer, the ones she's never seen — necks craned and eyes wide.

She doesn't know how long they've been there, and neither do they. On the roof, in the night, without walls and brushing up against one another, they are closer and more isolated than ever.

Maria looks across the streets, down the avenues, toward the jagged spine of Manhattan, similar scenes playing out on every rooftop in Brooklyn. Thousands of dreams, calling out to the veiled, screaming starlight.

Thousands of dreams, falling on the deaf ears of the universe.

"I wish tonight…"

There shouldn't be stars in Bushwick, but there they are.

There they are.

# Wednesday
# THE MYSTERY *of* THE GARBANZO BEAN MOROCCAN

## By Dave Medd

"THE MYSTERY of the Garbanzo Bean Moroccan with Toasted Pine Nuts" is what he'd call it, though a conventional reader would be content with the original title: "Curried Chick Pea Soup." Gareth had a rather novel approach to reading cookbooks — and he did indeed *read* them, not refer to them. It's not that he was a talented and devoted cook (he was, in fact, neither/nor), he simply found them pleasing reading as others may find a morning paper, the afternoon mail or an evening's Poe (not too late in the evening on the Poe, though, especially after an overly sauced pudding).

When Gareth turned to a recipe, the bookmark would immediately cover some ingredients. The title was mentally rewritten, punched up, made catchy for the reader's attention. A glance through the remaining ingredients revealed the clues: $\frac{1}{3}$ cup flour. "Indeed," thought the inspector, "this could be a misleading roux. Clearly not enough flour for baking, but certainly enough to thicken any plot." A half cup of cream (substitute $\frac{1}{3}$ cup plain yogourt). Ah, rich. Money could be a motive.

After ruminations on the evidence at his disposal — some still carefully hidden from view by the bookmark — it was on to the story itself.

1. Dice the onions and fry in 1 tbsp of the olive oil over medium heat until golden.

Onions! These had been hidden, new to his reading of the Garbanzo Mystery. Perhaps tears had been shed. A possible matter of the heart. But what did this mean for the richness of the cream? Love feigned in pursuit of money? Dastardly.

2. Add the remaining 2 tbsp of olive oil and garbanzo beans, stirring to coat beans in oil.

Vaguely erotic? Possibly; but with garbanzo beans? Earthy. That's it, earthy. A good, grounded man, stout of character though modest of means is beset by a beautiful, exotic, dangerous stranger (curry *will* come into this; Gareth had already seen the turmeric writing on the wall).

And so it would go. Each recipe step added to or altered what had come before as the story took form. The true challenge was always the ending. What does one do with "Simmer for 20 minutes" or "Bake 40-45 minutes?" Clichés all! Ending with whimpers, not bangs. Truly, who *simmers* to a satisfying climax, anyway? Maybe a slow build could work here after all, in a mystery involving an earthy Moroccan's toasted pine nuts.

But it's "Cook until done" that leaves the creativity clearly in his court and leads to the most fun.

Once the ending is resolved and Gareth's imagination purged for the evening, the cookbook is shelved in the kitchen or returned to the bedside table and he reflects briefly on how the story went as he tucks himself in. If pleased with it, he pictures a review or two in his mind's eye and damns the critics. "Written with all the artistry and originality of an onion soup recipe." Hypocrite! It's not like his precious, precise 748-word review didn't have its own carefully planned beginning, middle and end, the ever repeated three-part structure. Hypocritical glass-house living, stone-pitching bastards. Can't even distinguish a chicken stock story from a beef stock one.

# *Thursday*
# TYRANT'S JUSTICE

## By Brandon Crilly

A CHILL settled over his heart as he stepped into the plaza.

The spacious pavilion outside the Court of High Justice was empty as Keith began the long walk to the holding centre on the west side. Granted, it was nearly 10 o'clock at night, but he had assumed that people would still be out to see the attraction.

He was thankful that he was wrong.

Imposing buildings loomed on either side, as though the power of the Court itself cast long shadows over the ground below, dimming the yellow glaze of the streetlights. Even the rows of flags jutting from the rooftops were drooping, concealing the country's coat of arms. The oppressive darkness of the plaza matched the feelings that had settled over Keith during his journey into the capital.

Despite the dark, he could already see his destination at the far end; the shiny, metal cage was hard to miss in any lighting.

Papers were strewn across the decorated tile of the plaza, discarded by citizens during the day. He knew what each of the identical leaflets said without having to look. He had agonized over one throughout the entire day. He knew the fury embedded in the words, the anguish in the hands of those reading, and the bitter sense of victory in throwing the paper to the ground. He had gone through the same emotions over and over that day, though reaching a different conclusion. His was not the usual reaction to the capture of a mass murderer.

Every citizen knew about the crimes of ex-politician Felicity Ronnex. The media called her a "deranged psychopath" who had brainwashed her followers into turning against their government. Many suggested the atrocities she committed — seizing power, eliminating the former Prime Minister and then launching a war against the country's southern neighbour — warranted a slow, painful execution. Others suggested permanent exile to an isolated prison facility, which had been the fate of several of her rivals. A select few proposed that she was merely a reactionary in a country that was already decaying. Everyone celebrated Felicity Ronnex's capture as salvation from terror, and agreed she should be severely punished for her crimes.

Keith had watched the Court's debates all week in silence, trying to sort out his feelings. He finally decided he couldn't remain at home. The long train ride and the slow walk from the station had led him here.

The law stated that the worst criminals were to be caged outside so the public could express their outrage in person. The metal enclosure in the plaza had been in place for six days, allowing tens of thousands to face the accused. Keith did not agree with such practices. He could see scraps of refuse covering the bars and the ground of the cage, both inside and out. There were shards of glass and metal mixed with crumpled papers, rotted vegetables, and tiny squares of coloured confetti, the aftermath of nearly a week of passionate demonstration. The crude cot and washstand inside had also been coated with debris, tainting the few basic comforts the prisoner had been allowed.

Such was the expression of the country's fury.

He halted four metres from the bars, unwilling to step any closer. The cold in his heart had begun to numb his entire body, like a poison slowly eating him alive. He suppressed a shiver, forced himself to look through the bars at the figure within.

He hadn't seen Felicity Ronnex in person in three years. Instead of the powerful, domineering woman he remembered, he saw a thin frame hunched over a cot, a withered body covered in torn rags. Her long hair was dirty and matted, interlaced with bits of garbage she hadn't bothered to remove. There were scars on her hands, likely inflicted by her guards, and a single slash on one cheek from the first attempt on her life. Keith wondered why the Court hadn't removed her trademark piece of jewelry, a golden brooch showing a long-necked goose in flight, pinned above her breast. He remembered the Court had declared that emblem a mark of treachery a few days earlier.

The fearsome politician accused of assassinations, warmongering and other atrocities, was nowhere to be seen. Inside the cage was simply a defeated woman awaiting her sentence, trapped in the cold silence of the night. It was a pitying sight, one Keith had not been expecting.

He stood before the metal bars, unmoving and silent. He had considered several things to say, but nothing that he had practiced in his head seemed adequate. Nothing would give him the liberation he desperately needed. Keith examined the battered, emaciated figure, not sure if she was even aware that he had approached. He finally decided that any release had already been granted by the sight of the woman in the cage.

So he simply said, "Goodbye, Mom."

# *Friday*
# PLANTING FLOWERS

## By Celynne Grewe-Hinzmann

BARB SIGHS, and straightens her stiff back. She gives the tub one more rinse for good measure, then shuts off the water and puts the shower head back in its cradle. She looks around the bathroom critically, thinks it couldn't be any cleaner if it was run through an autoclave, and knows it won't pass muster anyways. She closes her eyes and sighs again. A whole weekend. She needs a glass of wine.

She checks the fridge over carefully as she takes out the Chardonnay. Looks good. Perfect in fact. She re-checks the fridge as she puts the bottle back after pouring a large glass. Then she opens the fridge again, removes the wine bottle, carries it out the back door and puts in the trunk of her car. It'll be easier to deal with the cops (if she has to) than with teetotaller Mom.

She walks slowly through the small house with the glass in her hand, giving each room a final inspection. The place looks immaculate, and she's proud of all her hard work. Barb is very handy, and artistic, always working on some new project, or three, and she's very grateful to Mom for instilling her with this vigour and enterprise. Her quaint little house and gardens are beautiful, the envy of the neighbours and her many friends. But there's no keeping up with Mom, so Barb's been working like a mad woman for the past two weeks getting everything in even more perfect form for this visit.

At sixty-seven, Dorrie Stevens runs circles around people half her age. She operates a fifty-acre working farm with a century house that she renovates perpetually, teaches yoga, music, ESL and painting classes, conducts the church choir, volunteers at the seniors' centre, the food bank, and the youth centre, takes care of her ninety-two-year-old mother, and is president of the Horticultural Society. And visits her daughter. For a whole weekend. Barb goes back out to the car and pours another glass of wine.

~

The doorbell rings at 7 a.m., sharp. Not 6:56 or 7:02. Barb wonders if she stands on the porch and watches her watch with her finger poised over the bell. But Barb's ready. Well, as ready as she ever will be. She was up at five, showered, cleaned the bathroom again, got her hair and makeup salon perfect, dressed in her best, tidied the bedroom and even scrubbed the kitchen floor, again, after breakfast.

"Mom! How nice to see you!" Barb smiles widely and gives her Mom a big hug, which is returned twice over.

"Hello, sweetheart! You look fabulous, dear! That shade of blonde washes you out a little, but what a darling cut. Pixie? I haven't seen one of those in years, practical though I suppose." Dorrie smiles brightly. "I see you finally got around to painting that old wicker porch set, what an interesting shade of yellow, but what on earth happened to your flower bed, dear?"

Barb grimaces. *Damn, how could I have forgotten to check that this morning!* "Oh, it's that darn little Nancy from next door. She loves to play in the dirt. Don't worry about that, Mom, I'll deal with it later." Barb reinforces her smile. Her cheeks hurt. "Come on in, Mom, I've got your room all ready. I'm so sorry I couldn't take the day off work, but we'll have a nice visit for the rest of the weekend. Now I want you to just relax today. Take a book, sit on the back patio and put your feet up for a change."

"Oh, don't worry about me, I'll find plenty to keep myself amused, dear." Dorrie chirps. "I know how busy things are for a teacher the last couple of weeks of school, I'm sure you're swamped. Though back in my days we had to write out all those report cards by hand, but I'm sure even with computers and all those canned comments it's still an enormous chore. Have you had breakfast yet?"

"Yes, but why don't I fix you something?" Barb's smile is threatening to crack her face.

"Don't you bother at all dear, I'll find myself something. You go and get yourself ready for work."

Barb forces her eyes to keep from rolling, decides to take the reprieve and retreats to her bedroom for a few moments to talk herself down. *I **can** do this.* When she re-appears several minutes later, the coffee is brewing, the bacon she didn't even have in the fridge is frying, and the orange juice is being squeezed.

"Can I fix you a couple of eggs?" Dorrie is wearing an apron and wielding a spatula.

"Thanks, Mom, but I had some granola earlier. I make my own, it's all organic." Did that sound defensive? It felt defensive.

"Well, at least have some juice. I brought some oranges, nothing like fresh juice. Thin girls like you need to be careful to get your vitamins."

*Let it go,* Barb thinks as she takes the glass being held in front of her. Mercifully it's time for her to leave. Mom sees her to the back door. "Now really, Mom, please just relax today. I'll pick up some nice steaks to barbeque for dinner, so don't fuss at all."

"Don't give me another thought, dear. I brought fresh vegetables from my garden for a nice salad for dinner and I'll get to that flower bed out front, after I defrost the fridge."

"Mom, really, I..." Barb grits her teeth. "I really appreciate that. Thank you." She escapes, hoping the car radio will drown out her screams on the drive to work.

~

Dorrie is hanging out the freshly laundered living room curtains on the clothesline when the back porch screen of the house next door opens, and a little blonde girl in shorts and a T-shirt comes out holding a popsicle in her chubby fist.

Dorrie waves gaily. "Yoo-hoo, Nancy, dear." The little girl looks around curiously, and then back at the lady. "I'm Dorrie, Barb's mommy. It's so nice to meet you. I understand you like flowers." The little girl nods at her blankly.

"Well, maybe you'd like to help me plant some?" The girl brightens. She nods happily and comes running over. The pair get gloves and trowels from Barb's garage and head to the front yard. Dorrie patiently explains all the fine details of planting flowers, getting the girl to help her dig new holes and smooth the cool earth around the root-balls, tells her the name of all the flowers and points out the shape and form of each variety. She talks about the importance of balance and scale to her mesmerized, obedient audience, how each plant has its own peculiarities and requirements for light, nutrition and water. When the bed is finally transformed, Dorrie takes her little charge by the hand.

"Well, doesn't that look nice? Thank you for helping me, and now you can see how much work it is to put all those flowers back, can't you?" The little girl nods seriously. "Good, time for a little treat then. Shall we have a tea party out on the back patio?"

Dorrie brings a china tea pot filled with fresh squeezed lemonade and a plate of the sugar cookies that she baked that morning out to the patio table on a silver serving tray. The little girl is delighted, enthralled with her beautiful new fairy godmother who knows all about flowers, lets her have three cookies and drink from a real tea cup, and she's sorry when her mother finally appears at the porch door to call her in.

"Hello, you must be Barbara's mother," her mommy calls to the wonderful lady. "I hope my little one hasn't been a bother?"

"Oh, no, not at all, we've had a lovely time!" Dorrie waves back.

"Well, thank you," her mommy says. "Barb's invited us over for coffee after dinner, we'll see you then. Come on in now, sweetie." The little girl slips off her seat and gives Dorrie a shy, quick hug before she runs home. Dorrie hums happily as she takes the tea things to the kitchen, and gets started on a lemon cake for the visit later.

~

The first thing Barb sees pulling in the driveway of her house, is the restored, improved, flower garden. *Oh, goodie.*

Dorrie is on the back patio, polishing silver and sipping lemonade. Barb knows it's homemade, and is suddenly, actually, looking forward to a glass. And wishing she could add vodka.

"Did you have a nice day, dear?" Dorrie asks as she pours.

Barb sinks into the patio chair, and gratefully takes the glass. "It was fine, thanks Mom, but not nearly as productive as yours, I see."

Dorrie laughs lightly. "Well, I do think I've solved your problems with Nancy. I had her over this afternoon, and got her to help me replant the garden. We had a lovely chat about all the different varieties, and the importance of respecting other people's property, and then we had lemonade and cookies as a nice positive reinforcement for all she had learned. Really, Barb, I'm surprised you hadn't thought of applying a little child psychology to the situation yourself, but I'm sure you won't have any more trouble with Nancy digging up the flowers."

Barb can't help it. She leans her head back and laughs out loud, long and glorious. "Oh, Mom," she finally manages, wiping the tears of mirth away with the back of her hand. "I'm so glad you had such a nice afternoon with Lisa. Nancy is her German Shepherd puppy."

# Week Two

"It's the way you ride the trail that counts."
— *Dale Evans*

# Week Two Authors

**Monday: Stadium**
**Larry Brown** lives in Brantford, Ontario. *Talk*, his first story collection, was published by Oberon Press in 2009, and *Satellite*, an ebook of flash fiction (including *Stadium*), is available at kobobooks.com. Larry teaches writing workshops throughout southwestern Ontario.

**Tuesday: Soldier's Last Wish**
**Phyllis Humby** lives in rural Camlachie, Ontario, where she indulges in her passion for writing suspense/thriller novels. Her stories, often scheming, twisted, or spooky, have been published in Canada, the U.S., and the U.K. In addition, she writes a humorous monthly opinion column, "Up Close and Personal" for *First Monday* magazine. **phyllishumby.blogspot.com facebook.com/TheWriteBreak**

**Wednesday: Consider the Suburbs II**
**Michael Milburn** teaches high school English in New Haven, Connecticut. He is the author of three books of poems, most recently *Carpe Something* (Word Press, 2012), and a book of essays. He lives in Hamden, Connecticut.

**Thursday: Time's a Wasting**
Originally from Toronto, **Nancy Boyce** and her husband John retired in 2011 to Big Bald Lake in the heart of the Kawarthas (Ontario). Nancy's first published story was on *CommuterLit* in May 2012. Since then Nancy has had a number of short stories published on *CommuterLit*, and in *Canadian Stories* and U.S.-based *Marco Polo*. When she's not volunteering in her community, Nancy can be found bicycling, kayaking or walking and playing with her dog Bailey.

**Friday: Missile**
**Kim Farleigh** has worked for aid agencies in three conflicts: Kosovo, Iraq and Palestine. He takes risks to get the experience required for writing. He likes fine wine, art, photography and bullfighting, which probably explains why this Australian lives in Madrid — although he wouldn't say no to living in a château in the French Alps. Eighty-eight of his stories have been accepted by seventy-four different magazines.

# *Monday*
# STADIUM

### By Larry Brown

THEY DON'T, won't allow it. I tell her that. She can buy one *at* the game. I tell her that too. All right, problem solved I tell her, I'll do it, at the game *I'll* buy you a sandwich. Diane, deep into another health kick — day two already! — slices the loaf of bread baked by monks or Mennonites, or maybe the Masons and their decoder rings. Stadium food, no, sorry, she's not about to go anywhere near stadium food. I tell her she's never been, not to a game, not to anything at the stadium, so the food there, what it's like, she can't, you know, *know*. Diane says she knows it'll be sausage this or sausage that and the sausage family is one food family she doesn't want anything to do with and besides, at the stadium any food that's not sausage-related might as well be sausage-related since what they put in it, well, nobody knows, nobody wants to know, just like you know what — sausage. I tell her there's a booth inside the stadium, it sells corn on the cob. Diane slices her skinless prairie-born-bred-and-beheaded chicken into thin strips. Diane says corn on the cob isn't a sandwich. I tell her corn on the cob is an example. Diane says corn on the cob, forget corn on the cob. I tell her corn on the cob, corn on the cob is proof. Diane says corn on the cob get off corn on the cob. Diane says corn on the cob? Diane says You're not making any sense. I tell her here's what's not making sense, right there on the counter, that sandwich. I tell her, *again*, they don't allow food, any food, to be brought into the stadium, *nyet* to outside food, we're not going to a potluck supper. Diane spoons mayo onto the chicken. She uses a soup spoon. Diane says me repeating myself doesn't make me right, me repeating myself makes me repetitive. I let go a noise, it's what a guffaw, a wet one, must sound like, I don't remember guffawing ever before. Diane replies with a noise of her own, a snort then a laugh with a scoff lurking inside. We sound like we share a cave. Diane says the security at the stadium, they'll turn a blind eye to her little snack, she's fine, she won't be pepper-sprayed. I tell her I've seen the security in action and that security, blind eyes there aren't any. Diane answers by wrapping her chicken-on-holy-bread sandwich in aluminum foil. Diane zips the wrapped sandwich inside a Ziplock bag, squeezes out every last spit of air. Diane opens the fridge and marches out the veggies. Dill pickles and their empire of sodium, I notice, she counts as a veggie. I tell her they're serious, the security people have to be, it's all this terrorism shit, the suicide bombers and everything like that happening all the time everywhere, and the world, it's not the same world nowadays. Diane wraps a double layer of aluminum foil around the veggies like she's shielding them from radiation. Diane says it's her mistake then. Diane says she's going to have to read the newspaper more carefully. Diane says she missed all the stories about Canada's corn on the cob stands being targeted by suicide bombers. What's next, soft pretzels? My God. Diane smirks. Maybe I smile. For sure I think a lot of things. Mayo and dills, I think, for instance. Diane asks if I'm ready. Are you? she says. Are you ready? she says. And I say, Are you?

## *Tuesday*
# SOLDIER'S LAST WISH

### By Phyllis Humby

THE SCREEN door opened. He crossed the threshold, his battle fatigues rumpled, and his black boots scuffed and dusty. His thickset chest heaved with emotion at the smell of floor wax and lemon oil. The eternal ticking of the round, white-framed clock goaded him forward. Shifting his brawny frame, a heavy boot cleared the floor. One tentative step led to another as he crossed the dimpled surface of the polished beige and red tiles.

He pulled the handle on the refrigerator door. The interior, spotlessly clean with scarred racks, held a mason jar of pickles, a can of Carnation milk, a saucer of butter, and an oblong casserole dish. The clear glass lid revealed leftover meatloaf. He seized the dish in one large hand and placed it on the linoleum counter, next to the mute radio with its black numbered dial.

Sliding the breadbox open, he reached inside for a partial loaf of Wonderbread. Unable to calm his tremor, the knife shuddered against the moist meatloaf as he cut a thick slice. The pungent smell of onions teased his taste buds. Swallowing back saliva, he placed the dense meat on a slice of plain bread. He knew where to find the mustard and slathered it across the other half of his sandwich.

Standing before the familiar cupboard, he reached for a small green plate, next to a stack of white dinnerware. A china cup with roses and faded gold edging disappeared in his grasp. Methodically, he filled the metal tea kettle with fresh cold water from the tap and carried it back to the stove. While the burner heated, he stood at ease, relishing the mundane task. Droplets of water trickled down the side of the pot, hissing and sputtering against the hot element.

A silver knife smeared with coagulated mustard remained on the breadcrumb-dotted countertop. His sandwich yet untouched lay within his reach. The canister of loose tea was left as he remembered, poised on a narrow shelf. He removed the lid. Tea leaves swirled from his meaty fingers, tumbling through the bubbling water.

A spike of awareness prickled his senses. He had no recollection of how he got home, only that it was a long way and he was tired. A vinyl-padded chair received his burly frame as he eased up to the chrome-edged table. The white cotton cloth, turned kitty corner, bunched beneath his elbow. Its colourful embroidered trim twisted with each movement of his arm.

Tea leaves gathered in the bottom of the misshapen strainer that was clinging to the top of his cup. Evaporated milk swirled the strong black tea into caramel as sprinkles of sugar disappeared beneath the surface of the steaming liquid.

He stirred slowly — carefully — before bringing the hot spoon to his mouth. One slurp of the scalding drink and the spoon clattered to his plate. Pursing his lips, he blew soft ripples across the surface of the tea, and then cautiously rested the edge of the cup on his lower lip for a small but satisfying sip.

He eyed the uncut sandwich that he held with both hands. Digestive juices flowed in anticipation, and within his body tinny echoes ricocheted. As he bit down on a crusty corner, his eyes squeezed shut at the familiar texture and flavour. A tear coursed through the stubble of whiskers leaving a salty wetness at the corner of his mouth. He took a second bite. The bread and filling rolled into a chewy mass as he savoured the taste and smell of home.

The clock's ominous ticking punctuated the unnatural silence of the room. Heedless, he basked in the peaceful setting. His gaze strayed, finally resting on the wallpaper pattern, faded cherries on a dull yellow background. His eyes fluttered to the woodwork, nicked and gouged. Every recognizable imperfection loosened the fist gripping his heart.

He tilted his head to the light bulb in the centre of the ceiling, remembering the warm glow of suppertime. The exhaustion ebbed. His tremulous hands grew still. He longed to look out the window but knew that nothing was there. This was all that existed. The realization of his yearning. The granting of his last wish.

## *Wednesday*
# CONSIDER THE SUBURBS II

By Michael Milburn

The morning throws up
mowing or sawing sounds,
rainwater tapping from
one gutter to a lower one,
and then leaves you to it,
just the occasional car
lapping along a wet road
a brushstroke for whatever genre
of mental painting you fancy.
In the city, I recall,
the cab horns would start up,
then the sanitation crashes
and the striding commuters
at non-negotiable hours
and you either fell in
or you didn't — I liked that, it was like the Army
or whatever milder version of the Army
helps a tentative guy like me
get up and at 'em, and stay distracted, if not calm,
and at least feel he's accomplished
something at the end of the day.
Suburbia purrs
to life, purrs all day
and cricket-creaks
to sleep, like a child's

bedtime book starring
round and interacting animals;
one needs to make
some hard decisions
to break out of its
feline schedule
and it's these decisions
that give this life its edge.
Out here you know that
starting at 5:30 p.m.
cars will slide
into their garages
like caskets onto
mausoleum shelves
and you won't be able
to face yourself if you're still
in your emotional nightgown
when they do, whereas at 73rd and 2nd
the night shift crosses the day shift
and the musicians are always
scrounging or heading for gigs. You pick
your demographic and convince yourself
that that's me putting my own spin
on getting by. Try
selling yourself
on being a gardener
or postman here in the land
of land pretending to no purpose
other than providing a staging ground
for your entrances and exits.
The machinery pauses.
That's your cue.

## *Thursday*
# TIME'S *a* WASTING

### By Nancy Boyce

THE CLOUDS hid the sun and a cold wind came up. I leaned into the wind, forcing myself to walk quickly. My puppy was learning how to heel and it helped if I kept a brisk pace. Icy rain stung my face, so I pulled up my hood, hunched my shoulders and stared down at the road ahead. I glanced up and saw snow swirling around my face, then noticed the ground was covered in snow and so was my puppy. I didn't understand how a snowstorm could come up so suddenly; it was only October. The clouds broke and a ray of warm sun shone through and the snow on the road began to melt. It stayed on my puppy's head making her look old and grey. I leaned down to brush the snow off her head, but it remained streaked. My hands looked more veined as if I was suddenly older too; perhaps it was the cold air.

Something was wrong, everything around me was different. The orange and yellow leaves were gone and the trees were grey and bare. I raised my arm and looked at my strange coat. I didn't know this coat, I didn't know these pants, nor these boots. What was happening? I tried to walk faster, to get to the comfort of my home where everything would be familiar and safe. "C'mon Bailey, let's hurry." Bailey couldn't hurry, she chose to move slowly.

Finally, we approached our house. The garage door was open. I didn't recognize the car parked in the garage, but felt relieved to see my husband's pickup truck.

We walked into the house and frantically I called to my husband. I walked to the windows and saw him working down by the water. As I turned, I noticed how faded the sofa cushions were. I had just bought them this summer, was so pleased with how they brightened up the room.

I was confused and exhausted. I lay on my bed and pulled the duvet up around me. Bailey snuggled in close to me. I stroked her fur and spoke to her softly. "What happened, Bailey? We were going to spend every day together and keep each other young. I wanted it to be different than it was with Sam. I wasn't going to wish for you to be grown up and calm. I was going to enjoy every moment of you being a puppy." I cried myself to sleep.

I dreamed vivid dreams; they seemed so real. I dreamed of our days together as if they were yesterday. Thanksgiving had just passed and we were making the rounds, saying goodbye to our cottager friends. Bailey was nine months old and full of energy. I released her and let her run to greet the neighbours. She ran circles around my friend's cottage and I egged her on with, "Run Bailey, run!" I let her have a quick swim and then we set off for our walk. I rewarded her at the end of the walk with a visit to another friend. We went into our friend's cottage and Bailey played with their dog. Then I let her run down the stairs and out to the water. She was having the time of her life.

I felt something slam into my chest. I had trouble breathing. My face felt wet. A bright light hurt my eyes, but I forced them to open.

My young Bailey was lying on my chest, licking my face, demanding that I get up and play.

My husband entered the room. "Are you two going to get up? It's a beautiful day, time's a wasting."

*Friday*
# MISSILE

### By Kim Farleigh

AN *LA TIMES* man looked across the plane's aisle and asked: "What are you going to be doing there?"

"Construction."

The hooked-nose journalist leant forward like an inquisitive eagle, curiosity crumbling in construction silence.

The heat covered the passengers like pelt suits.

The construction employee crossed over a defensive leg, and after removing a report and a felt pen from his brown, leather briefcase, he splashed green over white, tasks more alluring than people.

His hairline and sideboards were square. His brown, leather belt matched his brown, leather shoes, his reddish eyes dour in his reddish face.

The journalist contemplated simmering earth. Uncertainty resembles this heat haze, he thought. It would have been so easy to have just stayed in Amman.

Two NGO workers, a man and a woman, were beside each other on either side of the aisle, the man whispering: "He looks like a hung-over frog."

He was referring to the construction employee. His colleague's lips widened silently.

On the cabin-entry stairs, the NGO man had turned to wave to an empty desert, a "crowd" witnessing his departure, his friend's giggling engulfed by silence.

34

Shaved-headed security specialists were staring out the windows, khakis tight against their branch biceps, their necks thicker than normal arms, heads like bronze busts on their wide shoulders.

The female NGO worker whispered: "The brawn-brain ratio looks enormous."

"You're jealous because your arms aren't that thick," her associate replied.

The CNN journalist on the double back seat had blonde hair that looked hewn from satin and silk — like a beret with a split down one side. His black, mica eyes stared at the pilot who was glancing around, tapping fingertips in patient wait, the passengers still settling into their seats.

Black-and-white striped epaulettes sat on the pilot's shoulders. Dimples, like happy hoops, bracketed his wide mouth, his irises like stained-glass windows of amusement. The passengers sat facing him. Single seats lined the plane's fuselage, everybody apart in the narrow plane.

"A little manoeuvre may have to be done over Baghdad," the pilot said. "But don't worry." He chuckled, adding: "This is perfectly normal."

Lines covered his grinning face, like looking into a wind tunnel, his sea-blue eyes blazing like azure fires. "G-forces never hurt anyone's face," he continued. "Look at me: still gorgeous after all these years."

His opening hands expressed irrefutable logic.

The construction-industry employee's forced smile disappeared when he realized that the *LA Times* journalist was looking at him and smiling. The construction employee returned to his report.

"Enjoy the flight," the pilot said. *If you can,* he thought.

A chuckle escaped from the happy asylum of his thoughts as he returned to the cockpit where green fluorescence was shining upon instrument-panel black. The propellers started spinning. Cloud reflections deepened the depth of chrome propeller tips. The rushing desert blurred.

The plane's shadow rushed over a yellow world, dried-up-riverbed lashes suggesting that heat had inculcated itself into the land. Vehicles, like metallic beetles upon the asphalt strip that thinned where sky touched earth, fell off the desert's vast dish of scarred terrain.

The security employees were staring out windows, their mouths cleaved open by the tortuous luxury of boredom, distances now clear, heat haze non-existent from above.

Most of the passengers were reading, their heads down. The engines hushed.

A security specialist puffed his cheeks out; arching his back, he blew out. His companions smiled. One said: "Only an hour to go."

The passengers were absorbed by reports, newspapers, and magazines. The pilots' muffled voices rumbled over the purring engines. The flat, remorseless world remained unchanged.

"I saw an orange flash," the co-pilot said, "before his chute opened."

"Civilian aircraft bother me," the pilot said and smiled. "No ejector seats."

"We've been spoilt," the co-pilot said, grinning.

Another security specialist blew out while checking the time. The woman NGO worker turned a page of her magazine. She wasn't surprised that the security specialists were the only people on the plane not reading. Not intellectual types, she thought. It must be difficult for people like that to kill time. Probably never read a book between them. Her head turned rapidly so that she could lay her eyes quickly on the next page, her features set in pleasant contemplation. This happens when the future and the present seem new. She noted things in a notebook. Her ankle-length, floral-patterned, cotton dress covered her milky skin. Her red hair turned gold when caught by light, as if illuminating thoughts were firing up her follicles. Archipelago freckles dotted her cheeks' milky seas.

A security man ground his teeth together. His forehead became lined. His mouth, like a torn hole, grimaced with dull despair. His companions were still staring, without curiosity, out the windows, the distances clear — so clear that nothing seemed new — as clear as danger is to a trained man.

The redhead, turning pages, didn't see the desert becoming black earth. Buildings filled the blackness. Metal beetles, flashing like diamonds, glinted within the blackness, like cut glass on ivory.

The plane rose up. The journalists and the NGO workers looked up from their reading material. The aircraft started diving down — spiralling down! Facial expressions harmonized: eyes enchanted, mouths open, common expressions irrespective of education and intelligence, a unity of experience that wiped boredom's dryness from tired faces.

The sun flashed in the windows as the plane spiralled, a flashing sun like an ultraviolet atomic clock that ticked on objectively; the ground spun, faces pressed against cheekbones by G-forces...........it flashed past the right-wing tip — a silver bullet — smoke pouring out of its rear, its tip flashing in the sun.

The clefs of the woman NGO worker's lips unfurled to produce an oval encasing denture cliffs; she gasped: "My God!"

A thinning vapour trail underneath them became a cellular path of vaporous crocodile skin.

A security specialist said: "Don't worry. The pilots know how to avoid them. And there's only time for one."

His voice's unexpected softness didn't stop that alive hollowness from spiralling up her body like a malevolent spirit, swirling, entering her head, popping like fireworks, wiping out petty considerations, levelling self-esteem smooth. She clutched her rattling hands. She didn't even know this threat existed! Or that her body could create such chemicals, her sharp eyes glued to the wing.

The plane levelled out and landed. The strain left the passengers' cheeks. The desert had seemed too lifeless to contain deadly life — an illusion. The woman's heart slowed to a throbbing beat of relief.

A U.S. soldier, wearing desert khakis, and emerging from the desert background, appeared to have broken away from the land. Nothing had suggested that he had been in that wilderness. But he suddenly came into focus, as if the hazy heat, gyrating like a stewing broth above the ground, had given birth to life. The soldier's creation from this flailing atmosphere was so unexpected that his appearance seemed like magic evolution; not there; then he was.

"Are you okay?" the security specialist asked the woman. The man's eyes were kind. Before, he had just been a thick-necked ape.

"I wasn't expecting that," she said. "Thanks."

"No problem," he replied.

He felt amused because he felt he hadn't done anything.

"What are you going to do here?" she asked.

His gentleness was magnified by physical strength. He was younger than she had imagined. That gentleness looked amazing in that strength. His eyes now possessed surprising, alert kindness.

"We'll be looking after certain people," he said.

"You already have," she replied.

His grin's pleasantness resembled a fresh awakening.

The heat reached all parts of their bodies. They could feel it on the tips of their noses, and on their earlobes, heat capable of touching any place.

The soldier took them across the tarmac and into the arrival lounge, his face punctured by opal slithers of green friendliness. The M-16 he was carrying was a strange anomaly under the taffeta-like purity of his face; but his body was covered by white, green and brown patches that made this being of supposed innocence impossible to detect in the desert that stretched ever so slightly upwards to meet the sky's cobalt light that rose over those speck-like hominids. In that magnitude, they became ants in a place where few of their colony were prepared to go.

The woman NGO worker had never felt so small. Desert magnitude, she thought, creates positive smallness.

I now understand, she contemplated, how monotheism emerged from this landscape.

The construction-industry employee's smile was now natural as the male NGO worker said: "It was perfectly normal."

Amiability was a survival mechanism.

"Great job there," the woman told the pilot.

Her humble enthusiasm for others had never been so acute.

The *LA Times* journalist said: "It missed us by that much."

The CNN journalist said: "It ruffled my hair!"

The pilot said: "Hair-ruffling is perfectly normal here. Just look at Seth."

Seth was the co-pilot.

"My hair has been so ruffled recently," Seth said, "that straightening it out would be a waste of time."

The construction employee told the *LA Times* journalist: "I'll speak to my people about the *LA Times* doing some stories about us, okay?"

"Oh, great."

"Can you give me your contact details?"

"Sure."

The security specialist was asked by the NGO woman where he was going to be staying.

"The Green Zone," the security specialist replied.

"Me, too," she said.

His smile's brilliance made her response leap out of her mouth as if her comment had been fired out by air-compressed enthusiasm, his smile the device that had flicked open the lid.

"This is my card," she said. "If you don't contact me, soldier, I'll have you court martialed. That's an order."

"Yes, sir."

He erupted with titillated surprise, delighted with her ebullient audacity. Amazing strength emerged from her beautiful physical fragility. He gave her his card.

In the van that picked her up, she observed the security specialists getting into a Jeep.

"Caroline fell in love after the missile attack," her associate said. "Near death has altered her neurons."

"That," Caroline said, "is Hunk City, U.S.A. And it's going to be mine! Mine!! It's going to do whatever it wants to me in the name of security."

# Week Three

"In the name of God, stop a moment,
cease your work, look around you."
— *Leo Tolstoy*

# Week Three Authors

### Monday: Teaching

A semi-retired teacher, **Joan Vinall-Cox** currently lectures on storytelling and speaking, including podcasting, at the University of Toronto in Mississauga, Ontario. She is addicted to social media and reading detective novels. Her passionate love affair with words and curiosity about the puzzles of life propel her into poetry.

### Tuesday: The Hall

**Brad Gischia** was born in a small town in northern Michigan, and after he married his wife Kathy, they made the biggest move of his life, to the next town over. They have three children and a dog. Brad reviews, draws, and writes comic books and short stories in his free time, of which he has less every day. **comicwasteland52@gmail.com**

### Wednesday: Worm's-eye View

**Jan Wiezorek** writes from Chicago and teaches English to international students. His fiction has appeared in *The Bacon Review, FICTION on the WEB, Fanzine, Ozone Park Journal, Midwestern Gothic, TheWriteMag.com, Steel Toe Review,* and *PressboardPress.com*. He is author of *Awesome Art Projects That Spark Super Writing* (New York: Scholastic, 2011). Jan is an M.A. Composition/Writing candidate at Northeastern Illinois University. **teachwrite.net**

### Thursday: Crow Visits

Born and raised a Maritimer, **Catherine Sword** now lives in southern Ontario. Writing is the bookends of her life. She created stories in her youth and does so now as she approaches an end to a 25-year career as a librarian. She plans to explore the theme of poverty, which she began in a short story, "Bread" (*CommuterLit.com*) and in her novel, *The Poor House* (Wattpad.com).

### Friday: Planned Obsolescence

**Cassie McDaniel** was born in Texas, raised in Florida, and most recently adopted by Toronto. As a founding member of Soft Spot for the Universe writers' group, she has published fiction and poetry in *The Mangrove Review,* and the *Canadian Voices Anthology*. She makes other things too, including art and illustrations. **cassiemcdaniel.com**

# *Monday*
# TEACHING

By Joan Vinall-Cox

Everything is sharply edged,
richer,
more strongly felt,
like early love.

This task shapes
my beings and
my absences,
It wakes
my sleeping self
till I,
so I, am
ripe
for doing:

filled with my art
and ready.

# *Tuesday*
# THE HALL

## By Brad Gischia

JOEY WAS afraid to walk down the hall. I was uncertain as to where it had arisen, that fear, something that had sprung up almost overnight. We'd been in the kitchen after supper, cleaning up, and he was supposed to go to the bathroom. It was his routine, strictly enforced since potty training, but he would linger in the kitchen with "hey dad," and "I gotta tell you something…um," and me and Amy would get frustrated and threaten a time out or loss of television until he would get down there.

"Watch me down the hall?" It wasn't a question, not really, it was like a girl in a fifties monster flick asking to been seen to her door. It was expected of me as the dad, the all-powerful, strongest thing in the universe. And I would. Joey would reach up, fingers fumbling at the wall switch until light erupted from the fixture. He would twist his toes in the shaggish carpeting, the green walls bare but for a family picture. Two steps in and his motor revving high, rocketing across the carpet, feet thumping heavily to a chorus of "slow down" from Amy and I, until he was safely ensconced in the bathroom or his bedroom. Then it was fine.

We pondered the fear later. It wasn't the dark, not specifically anyway. I read somewhere that fear of the dark was fear of the unknown. No shit. Our ancestors were conditioned to be afraid because something in the dark was bound to eat you. I'm pretty sure it wasn't the dark with Joey.

He would turn the light on first, certainly, but it was the same for him at seven in the evening and nine in the morning. I was afraid of the dark when I was little. I remember the all-consuming fear, the irrationality of it all was clear to me even as I cowered beneath the covers, wakened from a nightmare, trying to get the courage up to whisper loudly for one of my parents to come and save me from whatever it was that I was afraid of. It didn't seem the same to me now.

So even though I was frustrated I tried to slow down, to understand what he was doing there, to comfort even when I knew it was irrational.

Last night we finished dinner a little early. We had tacos, it was easy clean up, just throw covers on the Tupperware and stack them in the fridge, so we were sitting in the living room with a cup of coffee when Joey started to kick at the carpet at the end of the hall, procrastinating, and something about the ease of the evening began to drain away.

"Just go, bud, there's nothing there."

"Will you watch me down the hall?"

"We're both here, just go." The news had just begun. Before I had children I never knew how nice it was to just sit and watch the news for half and hour, despite how depressing it usually is. The hall light clicked on, and he moved cautiously down one step, two, and then three rapid thumps towards the bathroom. Amy was intent on the anchorwoman. I looked down the hall. The bathroom light was off.

"Joe? Are you in the bathroom?" Nothing. Amy looked up, rolling her eyes at me, both of us knowing and dreading Joey when he decides to be stubborn, how long it will take to get him ready for bed and finally sleeping if he's not feeling helpful.

"Joey?" She stands; upset already, frustration creasing her brow, I can feel her ready to screech like a teapot as easily as if steam were shooting from her ears. I get up quickly.

"I've got it." She thumps back down heavily and zeros in on the news again.

I walk down the hall. The bathroom light is still off. No Joey sitting on the potty, mind in another world, humming or staring at the wall. His bedroom is quiet. Pete's bedroom is empty as well; he's still at the table pushing peas around his plate with the back of his fork and making motorcycle sounds. Our room holds nothing but the sleepy Bella, who looks up groggily at me and thumps her tail wearily.

"Joe?" We go through the house, angry, calling, warning, taking away TV, outside time, action figures, all the regular stuff when he's being difficult. I expect to see him huddled in a closet or down in the basement playing and completely ignoring our calls. Pete is undisturbed by us. The motorcycles have become bulldozers. Amy is soon frantic. Joey is gone.

The windows are all locked, the front door and back door as well. We primarily use the downstairs door because it opens on the garage. It's the only way he could have gotten out without us knowing; all the while I'm thinking that even that is impossible. *He was in the hallway.* For him to have gone downstairs, he would have had to pass by us in the time it took me to look from the hall to the television. I went outside. The yard was empty, the neighbourhood quiet in the early evening. Someone called for a dog three streets over. The birds sang in the late afternoon sun. I called a couple of times. Ran through the patch of woods behind our house and came out on the next street. Nothing.

When I came back inside Amy had the phone in her hand. I nodded. She called the police, who looked at us suspiciously from beneath their crewcuts and promised to check the neighbourhood even as they assured us he was probably next door or hiding somewhere in the house. They checked. Everywhere. No one saw him. Nobody saw anything remotely suspicious.

One night last week I awoke sweating in bed. I thought I heard Joey call for me. Amy found me an hour later tapping lightly on the walls of the hall asking for him softly, speaking

46

to the drywall and carpeting, pleading, hoping my scrabbling fingers would happen on a seam my eyes couldn't see, unlock a door without a key, find the button that would swing back the hidden room. The look on her face told me what she thought of my behaviour, a look filled with a kind of pitiful understanding that I hated. She went back to bed. I followed an hour later.

I don't know what happened to my son. The last time I saw him he was standing near the entrance of the hall, and I despair every time I think that I pushed him before he was ready, pushed him to take a step forward when everything in him was telling him to stay. I told him to go even when he wasn't sure, wasn't ready, before his five-year-olds' courage was strong enough. I remember that fear. It has been reborn in me with the loss of him. The fear of the dark and wild places that exist beneath our very feet, those places that can reach up and swallow us whole even when we believe we are safe.

# *Wednesday*
# WORM'S-EYE VIEW

### By Jan Wiezorek

I WAS looking through old black-and-white photographs in mom's album after she died, and she had saved my college shot of the lightning bolt hitting the campanile. It's a worm's-eye view looking up at the green oxidized roof. It shows the brightest, white-hot electric bolt I have ever seen. I took it with my pride and joy — the double-lens Yashica D. You can still buy that model today on eBay.

The charge came crashing down through the sky, spreading out sparks onto the tiled pyramid that topped the tower and its fifty-bell carillon. It was a fluke, I guess, that in the wind and rain I was able to take the shot at all — much less at just the right second to capture the stunning flash of light.

Just before the storm began that night, I was under the campanile with Cynthia Williams, my partner for the kiss. I think we both thought we'd do it just to say we did it rather than because we really liked each other. Tradition says we were supposed to kiss under the campanile at the stroke of midnight, but since we were there early — very early — we thought we'd kiss then. And we did, at 7 p.m., as the carillon's bells were chiming.

Cynthia said to me, "Michael, you're such a lousy kisser." Some lines I just don't forget — even if they do lack originality. I remember to this day her assessment of me.

We both parted in disappointment — she to the library and I to my voice lesson inside the campanile itself, which, I admit, was an odd place to rehearse. But Professor Timbers had her reasons. So, I opened the iron door-like grill at the base of the square limestone tower, more than 100 feet tall.

I called out: "Professor Timbers, it's Michael Donovan. I'm here for my lesson."

"Let's go," she replied. "You're three minutes late." I remember her voice carried down through the tower like thunder itself. It took me a few minutes to climb the metal stairs that rounded upward until I felt slightly dizzy at the top.

Professor Timbers, who played the carillon within the campanile, often rehearsed in the early evening. To save time, she sometimes scheduled voice lessons up there, too. She was wearing her typical black dress. She always wore black to school, and she reminded me of a recitalist preparing to sing in a jam-packed funeral parlour.

"Well, open your music; we're running out of time," she said to me, clearly disturbed. She sat at the carillon with its keyboard of levers that were attached to the bells. She would pound the levers with her hands and the pedals with her feet to create the bell concerts for which the college was well known.

She struck a lever that gave me a tinny starting note for my ballad. Unfortunately during my lesson, I stopped much too frequently for her. Whenever I asked a question, she was bothered tremendously. "Just try to get the note out, and support the voice with your diaphragm," she would say.

That evening, I stood near a small window inside the campanile during the lesson. Suddenly lightning hit, and the white light filled and then flickered within the tiny chamber atop the tower. Next, thunder piled on top of the roof, and I stopped singing once again to observe the torrent out the window — inquisitive and somewhat fearful of what could happen in such a storm.

"You're done. Just go," she said.

At first I wasn't sure what she meant. Eventually I said, "But my lesson isn't over."

"Go. The lesson's over," she replied. "You haven't the discipline."

"I'll focus on the music," I pleaded. She said nothing else, ignored me completely, and began to review her own music for next week's carillon concert. So, I sheepishly took my sheet music and camera and left. I climbed down the circular staircase, hearing thunder all the way.

Once outside, I was wet all over in seconds. But I reached up toward the rain, flashes of light, and thunder to take the shot. Just then, the bolt struck the patina-towered roof with catastrophic force. I didn't bracket my exposures or try for a better shot. Instead, I clicked this single picture into life.

# *Thursday*
# CROW VISITS

### By Catherine Sword

COLD AIR. Fly slow. Black wing shoves the still air, pushes body up. Up. See long. Roof. Roof. Tree. Stretch of grey solid ground. Tree with sparse leaves. Bank towards tree.

Car. Car. Car. Row of fence. Soft spruce tree. Tip wing, break through the chill, swoop down. Down. Down, flip feet out, grab soft blue spruce bough. Bob on branch. Look. Look. Fence, small roof. Shimmering glass. No flicker on shimmering glass. See, peanut lady?

Door. Door closed.

Caw. You there? Caw? Tummy rumbles.

Slip and grab bough, grab branch lower.

Caw.

Door open. Cat? No. Peanut lady.

Weak bald wing with claw throw little peanut out into snow.

White snow. Tiny drops, little holes. See shadows, little holes. One hole. One peanut. Remember.

Hole under tree. Hole by pond. Hole, hole, hole by fence. Go, peanut lady. Go.

Door close.

Swoop. Skid. Brush light snow up against black feather. Cold crystals slip between feathers. Shake and waddle. Grace left in the sky. Waddle left, right. Beak dives into round shadows. Peanut. Peanut.

# *Friday*
# PLANNED OBSOLESCENCE

## By Cassie McDaniel

**del.icio.us**
keeper
of things
1,641 things, exact,
not for forgetting.
you remember –
i forget,
temporarily.
you the keeper
sell-out
sold your space
sold my 1,641 things
to yahoo of all the bastards
any yahoo beats the life
from anything
then beats it again.
keeper, sad, sad keeper
thin and wasting
more white space by the day
i beg you, stay.
on my knees and dirty socks
sweatpants, pasty skin
i beg you
the internet means nothing

if i can't shout about
the things i can't remember
the things that you would keep for me, you
my brain without a head, you,
metaphysical memory.

## Google Notifier

an envelope turns red
in the corner of my screen.
like a kiss, i receive it,
and blush –
only my screen sees,
only my screen knows
what i know,
and what google knows,
too.

## Logitech Webcam

you came home with your own software
which was charming at first
you were shaped like an eyeball
thought you were clever
i placed you high, up on my crt monitor
on your clumsy feet
and you looked down on me
night after night, watching me,
blinking.
you tried to tell me who i was
you tried to make me put myself all over the internet
but you never captured sound.
it wasn't enough. you were never enough.
you weren't even built-in, not then.
that incessant blinking.
i cut your cable, finally, so i wouldn't be tempted
as if there was ever anything you showed me
that i couldn't see myself.

**Rollerball Mouse**
if i could understand you
your body limb
with bones inside
i could fix you
when you stopped moving
uncap your insides
clean them off
roll smooth again.
if things were simpler
less el ee dee
and i understood
the click and the
double click
and the scroll wheel
we'd go
wherever we wanted.

# Week Four

"We dream of travels throughout the universe:
is not the universe within us?"
— *Novalis*

# Week Four Authors

**Monday: Honour Thy Roots**
**Gloria Jean Hansen** is a nurse/bluegrass musician/author from Elliot Lake, Ontario, though she grew up in Kipling, Ontario. She has written several novels, articles, newspaper columns, and songs. She will someday retire to a cabin by the river to write full time.

**Tuesday: Free at Last**
**Dianne Korchynski** considers herself fortunate to be from Winnipeg, centre of Turtle Island. She strongly believes that place shapes the way we experience the world. Over the years, Dianne's work has been broadcast on the CBC, performed at Fringe Festivals, and appeared in various publications. Recently she has been performing her poetry with live jazz.

**Wednesday: Speak Softly**
**Cathy Hendrix** is a recently retired French teacher with a great love of language and literature, be it classic, contemporary or her enduring favourite, fantasy. Drawing on life experiences as well as a rich imagination, she has written several short stories as well as an as-yet-unpublished fantasy novel, the first in a series. Cathy lives and writes full time in southern Ontario.

**Thursday: Lotus**
A native of Baysville, in Ontario's Muskoka region, **John Donlan** is a poetry editor with Brick Books. He spends half the year in Vancouver and the other half on 200 acres of bush near Godfrey, Ontario. His collections of poetry are *Domestic Economy* (Brick Books, 1990/1997), *Baysville* (House of Anansi Press, 1993), *Green Man* (Ronsdale Press, 1999), *Spirit Engine* (Brick Books, 2008), and *Call Me the Breeze* (Alfred Gustav Press, 2013). He was the 2012/2013 Barbara Moon Editorial Fellow at Massey College, University of Toronto. "Lotus" was first published in *The Antigonish Review*.

**Friday: Hey Miles, What's the Plan?**
**Frank T. Sikora** is a freelance graphic artist, writer, and substitute teacher in Franklin, Wisconsin. He is fortunate to have the perfect first reader for his stories — his wife, an English literature teacher who has been known to offer helpful and concise advice, such as, "It needs a middle, honey."

*Monday*
# HONOUR THY ROOTS

### By Gloria Jean Hansen

PURPLE WOOLLY buggerfly be damned! How she had
ever wound up with a fly fisherman was beyond her, but she
suspected it was the tequila. She shook her aching head — a
mistake, she quickly discovered — and tried to make sense of
the last twenty-four hours. Stepping onto the plane for a
much needed vacation, sitting next to a fellow on his way to
the Yukon, taking advantage of a couple of free drinks and
the rest of the trip blurred. She recalled the turbulence, a
staccato voice from the cockpit saying they would be making
an emergency landing, the extended layover in Winnipeg and
a photo of her dancing on a tabletop wearing nothing but a
fisherman's skimpy vest festooned with homemade flies.

"You alive in there?"

"Barely."

Death must be better than this godawful ringing in her
head. His voice didn't sound so bad, but be damned if she
could put a face to the voice. Rod. Yeah, his name was Rod.
She'd giggled that one to death on the plane, trying not to
laugh, having to excuse herself to finish her stifled guffaws in
the washroom. A fisherman named Rod? He was so busy
rhyming off the different flies he had tied in his lifetime —
globugs, pike flies, dry flies, wet flies, nymph flies, streamer
flies, woolly worm flies, flesh flies, bug flies and poppers —
that he hadn't noticed her discomfort as they exchanged

names. It was almost as laughable as the lady she had met in the baggage check area, six feet tall and half as wide named Tiny.

*Owwwww. Kill me now. Please.*

"What's all the moaning? Can I get you anything, darling?"

Darling? It was worse than she could imagine. She had lost a good part of the last day in her life, and only now was it coming back in bits and pieces. She splashed cold water on her face and peered into the mirror.

*Gloria, oh Gloria. What have you done this time?*

Visions of Mother rushed in, hands on hips, demanding to know where she had been all night, that there were chores to be done, and who did she think she was, getting above the roots of her raising, hanging around with that mucky muck crowd from the city. She didn't see them around trying to help run this farm, and maybe she should move out so she could be with them full time.

Well, she'd taken Mother up on that one, and left the farm, never to return for a few years. But she came back with a college degree and a solid job in an advertising firm in the city. Mother didn't complain so much when she handed her fat wads of money to help raise her kid sisters and brothers, but oh how bitter the battle had been before the job.

"Let me in and we'll check out the damage. You might have had one too many there, darling. You sure drank me and Al under the table."

*ONE too many?* She felt like she had consumed the entire blue agave forest in Guadalajara and maybe the whole of Mexico. When the margarita mix had run out, Tequila Sunrises took over, and finally tequila, straight from the bottle, worm and all.

As she patted her face dry, something sparkled in the mirror. A ring? Nope. TWO rings. A whopping diamond and its mate. Oh, God. A wedding ring. She grabbed the towel bar for support. Really, the most out-of-character thing she'd ever done since leaving the farm was a teeny butterfly tattoo on her behind, and to date she'd almost forgotten about that weekend.

Come to think of it, tequila was involved then too. But married? Couldn't be.

"Are you nearly ready, darling? We've got another plane to catch."

"We? Are you kidding me? You and I aren't even headed to the same place! Aren't you going to the Yukon?"

"Yep. So are you, sweetie. I couldn't leave my wife behind. Come on out. I just ordered us some breakfast. Al's coming to join us."

Oh Sweet Jesus, it was true. Why couldn't she remember that part? She dragged herself to the door and opened it. There he stood in all his splendour. Her new husband. Not bad, easy on the eye, little older than she would have chosen, but trim and fit. And in far better shape this morning than she was.

"How? Where? When did we do this?" She held up her hand.

"Well, that part was easy. My buddy? Al? The one on the plane? So happens he's a JP. Don't worry, it's legal. Here. You signed the papers yourself. I wanted to wait until we had at least landed, but you insisted. We got the rings in the airport. You chose them. Please tell me you're not sorry. I have never done anything like this in my life, but I would do it over again. I called Mom. She's getting our room ready. I told her we'd be back in a week, that we were going on a fishing trip for our honeymoon, just like you insisted when you put my vest on. You are one hot babe when you get going!"

"Wait a cotton-pickin' minute here. We're going back to WHERE to live with Mom?"

"Rankin Inlet. I just took this trip south to pick up supplies for my business, Rod's Fly-By Fish Flies. I also write for *Outdoor Canada*, and they sent me on the trip to the Yukon.

So me, you and my buddy Al will be leaving soon. Let's go, get dressed. You can't wear that vest on the plane. I mean I don't mind it, but…"

"Shut up, Rod. I don't even know you. I am not going on any fly fishing trip, and I am going to find a way to undo this wedding. Annulment. Yeah that's what they do when a marriage hasn't been consummated. So we'll get an annulment. Here are the rings back."

"Sorry, sweetheart. It's been consummated," he said with a wide grin. "In fact you said you hoped we'd made a baby, and I told Mom she was likely going to be a grandma already. You really don't remember last night? You made me a happy man, darling. And that cute little butterfly…"

*Hose Cuervo, I hate you.*

"Sorry Rod. I am going in to pop a couple of Tylenol, take a shower and go home. I mean home. All the way home to my mother, so I can let her yell at me and tell me how stupid I am and that there are plenty of young farmers around, and why would I go off and marry some fly fisherman from Rankin Inlet…"

"Too late. I found her number in your wallet. She is ecstatic, her and the church ladies are already planning a reception for us when we get back from our honeymoon. She's even got a date lined up for Al. She's quite the lady, darling. Come here. Give us a kiss, Mrs. Rod Pike."

*Yes, God. Please kill me now. Right now. Stat. Immediately …*

## *Tuesday*
# FREE AT LAST

### By Dianne Korchynski

Adios dangerous kimonos
And other
High risk women's clothes
Daring you to stand
By a stove, your rightful, only, place
Salut you saris
Invitations to immolation
Adieu corsets wound tight
As golf balls
Squeezing the air right
Out of you
And those overly girded loins
Poured into girdles
Full to bursting
Ready like luscious breasts
To be released
Run wild — but not so, forgive me,
Titillating as they
But courting  a danger all their own
Au revoir crippled crumpled feet
That cannot be walked upon
Only admired
When shown
Their grotesquery encased in red satin

For that was then and far away
And this is now and here where
Shoes or clothes pose
No danger
No damage to body or bone
No danger
A hundred tiny bones squeezed into
High heel molds like bayonets self inflicted both weapon and
wound
No danger
From the harnesses holding in, propping up
Glued onto our very weary public breasts
No danger any more
Arrivederci
And welcome
The niqab, burqa, hajib
No danger, no danger

# *Wednesday*
# SPEAK SOFTLY

## By Cathy Hendrix

*IS THAT someone at the door?* Mary turned down the volume of the small TV that, due to her slight hearing loss, she had cranked to a level where she could comfortably hear Oprah's interview with that new young starlet.

Yes! Someone was knocking on her front door. Rather insistently to boot. Mary wiped her wet hands on the dish towel as she walked through the front hall. She could see the outline of a person through the frosted glass: colours — red top, blue — probably jeans — on the bottom, short blonde hair. *Oh no!* Mary's stomach clenched. *What does Pam want?* A thought flitted through her mind. Could she get away with not answering the door? She glanced at the entrance to the family room, mere yards away. Did she have the nerve? Too late. Pam had seen her. Mary grasped the doorknob, forced a smile on her face, and opened the door.

"Pam! Hi!" she said, hopefully inviting a pleasant, or at least non-confrontational, response from her next-door neighbour.

Pam stared at her, the corners of her mouth drawn down, giving her quite attractive face a rather pinched and, to Mary's mind, self-important expression. One fist rested on the curve of her slender hips, giving no room for mis-interpreting her mood.

After several uncomfortably silent moments, Pam replied. "I have something for you." She turned and picked up a shoebox from the porch behind her feet.

Mary frowned. Something for me? This can't be good. As she caught a glimpse of what was resting in the shoebox and then a whiff of the most unmistakable odour, Mary knew. She sighed.

"Pam, Buster has been in the yard all day. It must have been another dog."

"Oh? I don't think so! I know Amber took him for a walk this morning. I saw her leaving when I got the morning paper. I think she did it on purpose! She doesn't like me. I know it! Not since that incident with the police."

Mary pinched the bridge of her nose. She'd prefer not to dredge up that unpleasantness. Nothing was easy with Pam. "Look, I'm really sorry. I'll speak to her and find out what happened. But believe me, she'd never let Buster do it on purpose."

Pam's nostrils flared. "I just might have to call the police again if this continues. My little Xavier is only four. My baby could have stepped in this, if I hadn't been watchful."

*Well that would never happen, now would it? You never let your kid get more than two feet from you. Ever. You'd think he was made out of porcelain.*

"Well, as I said, I'll speak to Amber." Mary put on her best commiserating smile. "Wait till Xavier's a teenager. Suddenly they have attitude and don't pay attention to 'unimportant' things like what the dog is up to."

"Hmph. Any mother worth her salt would teach her child right from wrong!" Without another word, Pam turned and stomped down the stairs, disappearing behind a shrub on the way to her home.

"What did the bat lady want?"

Mary turned at the sound of her daughter's voice. Long chestnut hair, perfectly straightened, surrounded Amber's pretty face. *She'd be even prettier if she'd stop scowling all the time,* Mary thought. "Did Buster poop on the Pipers' lawn this morning?"

Amber shrugged. "I dunno. That bitch is never happy. If Buster did, then good for him. She deserves it after calling the police on me."

"Amber, don't provoke her. She could cause you and me a lot of trouble. She's that kind of person."

"Oh Mom, get some backbone!" Amber came down the remaining three steps and stood in front of Mary. "She only picks on you because you let her."

Amber's eyes shifted to her hand where her phone had begun to blare some unintelligible pop song. She immediately put it to her ear and turned away, already deep into conversation with one of her myriad friends. Just before she disappeared into the family room, she whisked around and said, "Oh, I need the car tonight. Jen's having a party."

Mary stood alone in the front hall holding the shoebox. The revolting aroma was threatening to permeate the entire house. She grimaced, and quickly went through the door to the garage where she disposed of the evidence. As she walked back to the kitchen, she realized that her head had begun to pound. Her shoulders sagged. *It must be the humidity. Everyone gets cranky when they're hot.* With a heavy sigh, she went back to preparing dinner.

~

"Is this dinner?" Bob demanded as he sat down at the table. "My mother made me eat meatloaf once a week all my life until I finally moved out. I can't stand the sight of it!"

"Your mom said it was your favourite," Mary said in dismay, her heart sinking. "You said you were sick and tired of our usual meals, so I thought I'd surprise you." In a smaller voice she added. "It's your mom's recipe."

Mary's hand hurt. She realized she'd been gripping her fork so tightly her knuckles were white. She deliberately set it down and put her hand in her lap. "But if you don't want it, I can make something else."

"Something else? I don't want to wait another hour to eat." Her husband looked sourly at his plate. "I'll have to eat it now if I don't want to starve."

"Pam came over and was yelling at mom again," Amber informed her father.

"What?" Bob's eyes flew up to glare at Mary. "What did she have to bitch about now?"

"Buster pooped on their lawn again." Mary could feel the headache returning.

"How could she know it was Buster? Did she see him?"

"Apparently she saw Amber taking him for a walk this morning."

Bob snorted. "Can't people take their dogs for a walk without her making a big deal? What did you tell her?"

"That I'd speak to Amber about being more mindful of what Buster's doing while she's walking him." She looked pointedly at her daughter.

"Me?" Amber's eyes opened wide. "I didn't do anything! That's the thanks I get for walking Buster? Mom, you should have stuck up for me!"

Mary's head felt like it was going to split open. She stood up and took her untouched plate to the counter, then walked out of the kitchen and out the front door. She needed some air. The early evening sun had cast everything in a warm golden light. She smiled at her red geraniums that marched proudly beside the garden walk over to the driveway. Then she frowned. Pam's husband Ray had obviously been cutting the grass. Huge sodden green clumps lay strewn all over Mary's newly sealed driveway. Anger suddenly bubbled up from somewhere deep down and filled her chest with a burning pressure. Turning into her garage, she snatched up a broom. *Tsking* with every sweep, she began

66

vigorously removing the unsightly mess, her hands squeezed tightly around the smooth wood of the broom handle.

*Crash!* Mary froze, then looked fearfully to her right. One of Pam's expensive flower pots that lined her side of Mary's driveway lay in shards on the grass, oozing soil and petunias.

"Oh my god! Look what you've done!" Pam shouted from her garage. She grabbed a broom that was hanging from a hook and hurried over to survey the damage. "Oh, my beautiful pot! Can't you be more careful?" Pam bent down and picked up two large pieces of blue ceramic pottery. "You're going to have to buy me a new one. I don't know if I'll be able to match it with the others now. If I can't, then I'll have to replace all three. You'll pay me for that!"

"Excuse me?" Mary couldn't believe what she was hearing. "All three? I don't think so!"

"That's so typical of you Mary Jansen. You never take responsibility for anything. Well, this is all your fault." Pam took an angry swipe at Mary's broom with her own.

Mary felt the hateful vibration transfer from the broom handle up into her wrists, and as far as her elbows. But it didn't stop there. The emotion that it carried seemed to aim straight for her heart. Mary gasped. Her hands gripped the broom handle convulsively, then, as if of their own volition, raised the broom and brought it down with a crack against Pam's. Pam let out a cry and jumped back. But only so she could raise her own broom to take a better swing.

A couple out for an evening stroll heard a strange clacking noise and stopped to gape at the two women who were fencing with brooms in the driveway across the street. They watched as the dark-haired woman's broom made contact with the blonde woman's shoulder. A loud shriek filled the peaceful evening. The broom handles were whizzing furiously now and both women were shrieking at each other. A cyclist pulled up beside the couple to watch. He winced as the brunette landed a solid blow on the blonde's head. Blood started to trickle down her face. He pulled out his cell phone.

~

Mary rubbed her forehead. It was cool and dim in the room. Her headache was finally disappearing. She sat back against the cinder block wall and looked around. It wasn't at all what she had imagined it would be. Not at all like on TV. The walls were painted pale yellow. The metal door with the small glass window was that grey-green institutional colour. The cot that she was sitting on at the moment was actually not uncomfortable. There were no bars to be seen. The silence in the tiny cell was heavenly.

Mary smiled and let out a soft sigh. Her shoulders straightened. Apparently Pam would be facing charges too, but not until she returned from the hospital. She grinned more widely, closed her eyes and imagined Bob's face in front of her as she wielded her mighty broom once again.

*What's that old saying about carrying a big stick?* Mary chuckled. *Well, it certainly beats speaking softly.*

# *Thursday*
# LOTUS

## By John Donlan

Today I spent too long breathing the scent
the wind carried across the water:
acres of white water lilies, thousands.
At the far shore

under the forest wall, they're dots;
here, they could be emblems
of enlightenment and perfect peace.
Disordered by their perfume,

I imagine this afternoon unending,
I jump the job, never to return,
while my colleagues drudge
and laugh that I call this work.

That's how far I am from enlightenment
and perfect peace. When I look out again
the lilies have closed against the sun,
fisted in green casings until tomorrow.

# *Friday*
# HEY MILES, WHAT'S
# THE PLAN?

## By Frank T. Sikora

MILES EDWARDS, sixty-seven, former outdoor life editor of the *Bismarck Tribune* and part-time substitute schoolteacher, entered room 134 of Bismarck High. Murmurs of recognition greeted him, punctuated by Stephanie Riley's squeal and then shout of "Miles! Yes!" While the students laughed, Stephanie poked her friend, Anna, and said, "See, I told you it would be him."

Miles waved and closed the door, temporarily sealing out the chaos behind him. As he walked to the podium, he thought *I should just go home. I should go home before the next onslaught of probability waves. I should go home before I break down in front of the kids.*

When Miles entered the school that morning, his gift — the ability to see the multitude of reality states and probable futures of an individual — had again turned dark and pessimistic. As he studied the kids' faces, he saw only lives of despair, futures filled with tragedy. *Lord*, he wondered, *what happened to the days when I not only saw the darkness in their lives but also the light?*

He couldn't leave, though. He and his wife needed the money. At his age, his job prospects had been reduced to substitute teaching or delivering newspapers. His 401(k) decimated; he and his wife needed the $80 per day to supplement their Social Security. Miles took little comfort knowing that in all his realities, the results were similar. The worldwide economic downturn raged across all his existences.

"Good morning, ladies and gentlemen," Miles said. The students playfully snickered when he wrote his name on the whiteboard with the honorific, "Mr." To the kids, he was Miles, and had been since the first time he subbed for Ms. Klusmeyer in her freshman English class. Stephanie had asked if she could call him "Miles," and looking out at the plump and sweet Ms Riley, he had said yes. Now he was known as Miles, nothing more.

Miles gazed at the students, starting to his left. It was a relief to see Janet Hastings looking well. He recalled seeing nothing but doomed futures for her the last time he taught: childhood leukemia, traffic accidents, drugs and poverty. It was as if the universes had a malicious vendetta against the poor girl. He quickly turned away, afraid to look closer. For now, he could convince himself she would be safe.

Stephanie raised her hand. "Hey, Miles, what's the plan?"

When Miles turned toward the student, one of his favourites, a sickness slithered in his gut. He hadn't noticed before, but the young redhead wore a Goth-inspired ensemble: black scarf, black T-shirt, black socks, shoes and pants — an unusual colour palette for the girl whose current reality states rarely involved anything more serious than classroom anxieties, troubled romances, and family disputes. Although he recalled her probable futures as being mostly cloudy, Miles had not worried about this because his visions were often unclear and shifting in nature — clarity was not a given. Now darker harbingers gathered around the girl, each one fighting for prominence and each one shaded with predatory undertones.

Miles shuddered. He felt a protective affection for the girl as a parent might have for a favoured and awkward child.

Despite her good nature, he had sensed loneliness within her, which transcended all her possible lives.

"Miles?" Stephanie said with a wave. "Our assignment?"

"Yes, the plan," Miles stammered. He flipped through his notebook for Klusmeyer's instructions. "The plan, the plan," he said, forcing a smile. "Well, Stephanie, it appears you have a pop quiz on chapter three of Steinbeck's *The Red Pony*. Ah, one of my favourite Steinbeck works."

The students groaned.

"How about a movie instead?" Leo Mazano asked.

Miles turned to the thin, dark-haired boy sitting in the second row by the windows. The morning light slipping through the half-drawn shades illuminated the boy's dull, grey eyes. The beast in Miles's gut dug deeper. He saw needle tracks along the boy's thin arms, and Mazano lying prone and alone on a worn and filthy bed. He saw a father, a man buried in anger, wielding a belt on the cowering boy. He saw the boy handcuffed and led away by police.

"Jesus," Miles uttered. Must all their lives be consumed with hopelessness? What have they done to incur the wrath of all the universes?

"Yes, a movie," Stephanie said. "A Pixar."

Miles shook his head. "A movie? No, not today. I'm sorry. We must complete our assigned tasks. Test conditions, please. Books on the floor and no cell phones. I trust you've kept them in your locker."

"Oh, Miles," Stephanie said, "you're breaking our hearts."

And you, mine, Miles thought.

~

During his lunch break, Miles sought refuge in the library, finding an empty cubbyhole buried behind the periodicals, hidden by the lonely shelves of science and geographic magazines. Whispers hung in the air; their masters unseen. Even in the empty spaces free of children — and the kids were just children, knowing nothing of all the worlds and desires the universes held — probabilities haunted him.

He opened his book and read. He hoped seeking sanctuary in the familiar comfort of his favourite writers would drown out the din, and he'd find shelter in the arc of imagined lives.

He scanned the pages, but nothing emerged. The letters did not form words. They were only patterns — art forms without thought, without story.

He set aside the book.

The voices grew louder. Miles grimaced. He knew the speakers. He knew the kids. They screamed. They pleaded. They cowered under blades of angry indifference.

Stop. Please.

"Miles, what's wrong?"

Miles lifted his head, twisting toward the voice off to his right. It was Stephanie. He felt a thickness gather in his throat. He forced the words to form. "I'm not feeling well, Stephanie. Nothing more."

Stephanie glanced to her left and right and leaned close. "You've been crying," she said, each word carrying the weight of empathy.

"Old men get sad," Miles said. "Please don't tell. I wouldn't want to lose my reputation — you know, the biggest badass substitute in Bismarck."

Stephanie laughed. She also cried. She raged. Probability waves blinked in and out as if a line of Stephanie's were auditioning for a part in a play and quickly exiting off stage.

Miles felt as if he would break down into more tears. He had exposed too much already. The girl needed help, but he could not bear to bring himself to listen or watch. Ashamed of his weakness, Miles stood. "I must go, Stephanie. Sorry." He left without turning. No, he fled.

~

Students jammed the hallways as they left the cafeteria for their afternoon classes. Head down, with his workbag slung over his shoulder, Miles slipped through the torrent of kids. Students called out his name, but he neither stopped nor waved. The voices of those seen and unseen rose, building to a crescendo. Where can I find peace? Miles inwardly pleaded.

He approached his classroom. Stopping at the door, he considered leaving. At home, locked away in his den, he'd be safe. He could shut out all the worlds, or at least try.

He didn't. He never shirked a responsibility. His wife loved that about him. I am a stand-up guy, he thought bitterly. I always do what's right. What a fool…

He entered the classroom.

~

Stephanie stood in front of his desk, looking distant and small. "Miles, please don't run away from me. You once told us we could tell you anything. You were talking to the whole class, but I knew you meant me."

He couldn't recall the conversation, but that didn't mean it hadn't occurred. Lately he had problems separating the probable lives with the one being led. "You're right. I shouldn't have run away from you. Sorry."

Miles closed the door and checked the clock: Class would begin in 15 minutes, then the kids would file in and the probability waves would renew their assault. He remembered when he had loved his gift, when he had embraced all the possibilities the worlds offered. He had revelled in the richness of existence. He felt privileged to know its secrets. Now, all he saw was the crap a cruel and bitter world, no, worlds, had dumped on humanity, on these kids. Christ. He loved them. He didn't do this job for the money, not anymore. He did it because he cared for the kids, for the hope they held, blissfully unfazed in their hearts by all the brutality of the world.

Stephanie slipped to the floor. Her backpack landed with a sad thump. Her hair fell over her face and she shook and choked out soft sobs.

Miles rushed to her. He knelt close. "Stephanie, what's going on?"

She turned away and said softly, "I guess young girls get sad, too."

"Yes, and they lead secret lives, fiercely hiding them from all those who care about them," said Miles.

Stephanie nodded. She gathered a breath and spoke. Her words showered him like a meteor storm: all she had endured at the hands of her stepfather — the hopelessness, the degradation, and now the suicidal thoughts. She had carried the secret for years; it was her burden to carry, alone, and to hide.

How had I missed this? Miles lamented. What use is this gift if I can't see the reality in front of me?

Miles studied the girl.

She looked ready to fold in on herself, collapsing under the weight of her sadness. She saw only one future, one terrible end.

Miles smiled.

He understood his gift.

Finally.

He gently pulled on the girl's sleeve, guiding her up. "Come with me, Stephanie. Let's talk. I know you only see one outcome, one way out, but there are other possibilities. Trust me. You may not see them, but I do."

# Acknowledgements

A heartfelt thank you goes to the contributors to this anthology and to the readers and contributors to *CommuterLit.com*, for their enthusiam and support. This was truly a cooperative venture.

In particular, the editor would like to acknowledge the hard work and contributions of the following individuals:

Doug Bennet, for tech support, marketing advice, his design skills and moral support.

Brian Henry, of *Quick Brown Fox*, who has steered many good writers our way.

Frank T. Sikora, for his cover design advice.

Matt Webb, who designed the *CommuterLit* logo.

# An Invitation

Join the *CommuterLit* community of readers and writers — log on to *CommuterLit.com* daily and spice up your transit commute reading. And watch for the next issue of *CommuterLit Selections*, promoted on the website.